KIDS CAN'T STOP READING
THE *CHOOSE YOUR*
OWN ADVENTURE® STORIES!

"I like *CHOOSE YOUR OWN ADVENTURE*® books because they're full of surprises. I can't wait to read more."

—Cary Romanos, age 12

"Makes you think thoroughly before making a decision."

—Hassan Stevenson, age 11

"I read five different stories in one night and that's a record for me. The different endings are fun."

—Timmy Sullivan, age 9

"It's great fun! I like the idea of making my own decisions."

—Anthony Ziccardi, age 11

AND TEACHERS
LIKE THIS SERIES, TOO!

"We have read and reread, wore thin, loved, loaned, bought for others, and donated to school libraries, our *Choose Your Own Adventure*® books."

CHOOSE YOUR OWN ADVENTURE®—
AND MAKE READING MORE FUN!

Bantam Books in the Choose Your Own Adventure® Series
Ask your bookseller for the books you have missed

Choose Your Own Adventure® Books for younger readers

THE FORBIDDEN CASTLE

BY EDWARD PACKARD

ILLUSTRATED BY PAUL GRANGER

BANTAM BOOKS
TORONTO · NEW YORK · LONDON · SYDNEY

RL 4, IL Age 10 and up

THE FORBIDDEN CASTLE

A Bantam Book / August 1982
2nd printing ..... October 1982   3rd printing ... November 1982

Bantam Books are published by Bantam Books, Inc. Its trade-
mark, consisting of the words "Bantam Books" and the por-
trayal of a bantam, is Registered in U.S. Patent and Trademark
Office and in other countries. Marca Registrada. Bantam
Books, Inc., 666 Fifth Avenue, New York, New York 10103.

PRINTED IN THE UNITED STATES OF AMERICA

O   12 11 10 9 8 7 6 5 4

For Wells, with appreciation
And special thanks for the court of
Rufus the Mad

<u>WARNING!!!!</u>

Do not read this book straight through from beginning to end! It contains many different adventures you may have in medieval England and France as you search for the Forbidden Castle. From time to time as you read along, you will be asked to make decisions and choices. Some of them are dangerous!

What happens to you will be the result of your choices. *You* are responsible because *you* choose. After you make each choice, follow the instructions to see what happens to you next.

Think carefully before you make a decision. You could be stuck in medieval times forever—or you may find the Forbidden Castle and get back to the present time.

Good luck!

You promised yourself never to go back into the Cave of Time! But when you found the opening behind a big boulder in Red Creek Canyon, you couldn't resist.

The Cave seemed darker than before. You slipped and fell. Your head hit something. And here you are, lying in a field, looking up into the branches of a big oak tree, with no idea of where you are, or even what century it might be! Now you may never see your family and friends again.

Rubbing your aching head, you take in the scene around you. Nearby you see a narrow dirt road, and beyond it a fast-running brook. The road disappears into dense woods on either side of the field.

You hear the sound of hooves, and a strange clanking noise. *Someone is coming!* You duck behind a tree as two men on horseback ride toward you. They are wearing shining metal armor. One of them carries a white banner with a golden lion on it. They must be knights! You watch as they rein in their horses and dismount just a few yards away.

"It has been a long ride, Sir Rupert," says the taller one, "and you have had a long time to think. Tell me, have you solved the riddle of the Forbidden Castle?"

Go on to page 3.

"In truth, Sir Godfrey, I have tried, and so has everyone else in England. What a reward King Henry has offered—half the kingdom of Wales!"

"A handsome reward indeed," Sir Godfrey replies, "but not an over-generous one, for the old monk promised King Henry that if he conquered the Forbidden Castle he would rule all of Europe!"

The knights fill their flasks with water from the stream. As they walk back to their horses, Sir Godfrey says, "We must get on to Cotwin Castle. The king expects us before the sun passes behind the west tower. He will be angry if we are late."

"Aye," says Sir Rupert, as he vaults onto his horse. "The king has been in a fearsome temper since he learned that there have been foreign spies in the English court. And now he has ordered that all suspicious-looking travelers shall be locked in the dungeon!"

As the knights prepare to ride off, you wonder whether you should come out from behind the tree. You're wearing twentieth-century clothing. Surely you will look suspicious to these knights. On the other hand, you can't stay hidden forever.

If you decide it would be wiser to wait for the next passerby, turn to page 4.

If you decide to step out from your hiding place, turn to page 6.

You decide to wait. As the knights ride out of sight, you hear a deep voice behind you.

"Are you going to stand behind that tree all day?"

Turning, you look up into the eyes of a giant of a man. He is wearing leggings and a tunic made from deerskin. He holds a bow in one hand. A quiver filled with arrows is strapped over one shoulder.

"You don't want King Henry's knights to see you, eh?" He laughs and adds, "Then you are a friend to me. Those puppets give me more trouble than they are worth!" He bends down and looks closely at your face. "My word, I have never seen the likes of you in these woods!"

"I am a stranger from another place and another time," you say. "Could you tell me what year it is?"

The giant laughs again. "I don't keep count," he says, "and I have never seen why anyone should! Garth is my name, and you can stay with me, if you like."

"Where do you live?" you ask.

Garth answers with a wave of his arm. "My house is the whole wide forest! There is plenty of food, and plenty to do—it is the only place where a person can be free. Why not join me? Of course, if you are bothered by a little rain and wind now and then, you can follow that road to Cotwin Castle. They'll give you a roof over your head. I must warn you, though, it might be the roof of a dungeon."

If you decide to go with Garth, turn to page 7.

If you decide to try your luck at Cotwin Castle,
turn to page 9.

Just as the knights mount their horses, you step out from behind the tree.

"Who are you?" asks Sir Godfrey. "Where did you get those strange garments?"

"I know a spy when I see one," says Sir Rupert. He leans over and pulls you roughly up on his horse. "If this is not a spy, it is the devil!"

Sir Godfrey bring his horse up next to you and stares at you intently. "The devil is crafty, and knows how to assume an innocent form, but I will not be fooled! We'll take this devil to the castle, Rupert, and thence to the dungeon."

Turn to page 10.

You've always wanted to learn how to live in the wilderness. This seems like the perfect chance. You follow Garth as he leads you through pine forests, across roaring brooks, and up steep rock ledges. The sun has dipped below the western hills when you reach a shelter under a rock ledge. You help him gather sticks and pine boughs, and you are soon warming your hands before a blazing fire.

"Why do you live in the woods like this?" you ask.

He grins. "Ever since I told King Henry that he was no better a man than anyone else, he's had a price on my head. He has lost five of his best knights trying to bring me to the gallows."

"Before I met you, I overheard his knights talking about some riddle. Do you know anything about it?"

"Yes, and it is quite a story," says Garth. "About a year ago an old monk visited the king and told him about a mysterious castle. Of course, the king demanded to know where this castle is. But the monk would not tell. Instead, he recited a strange riddle and then said, 'Who solves the riddle will find the castle. And who conquers the castle will rule all Europe.'

"Ever since then, King Henry has been trying to solve the riddle. He is angry because none of his wise men can do so."

Go on to page 8.

8

"Do you know the answer to the riddle?"

Garth laughs. "I do not even know the riddle. If you want to find out, you must gain admittance to King Henry's court. You may succeed, but if they suspect you are a runaway serf, they will throw you in the dungeon."

You have no way of knowing what may lie in store at Cotwin Castle. But it's risky staying with Garth. He has said himself that the king's knights are searching for him.

If you decide to try your luck at Cotwin Castle, turn to page 12.

If you stay with Garth, turn to page 11.

You thank Garth for his offer, bid him farewell, and set out for Cotwin Castle.

You have not gone far when you see a woman coming down the road. She is hunched over—almost hidden by her black shawl—as she walks alongside a wooden cart loaded with hay and pulled by a little gray horse.

If you let her pass and continue on toward Cotwin Castle, turn to page 14.

If you stop the woman, turn to page 16.

10

You cling to the horse, trying to keep from falling off, as the knights gallop to the castle yard. They drag you down a long flight of crumbling stairs. One of them opens a creaking iron gate. Another shoves you into a dark, musty room. The gate swings shut behind you.

The floor of your new quarters is rock. There are no windows—only a few cracks in the walls that provide barely enough light for you to see your cellmate, crouching in the corner. He is very thin, and his grimy hair hangs halfway down to his hips.

"Keep away from me!" he shouts. "Your clothes were made by the devil. . . . Don't come near me!"

"Please don't be afraid. I won't hurt you. But do you know what they will do with me?"

"Most prisoners are beheaded, but if you are found guilty, they'll burn you at the stake. It is the only way to purge the devil from your soul!"

He steps closer. "Don't worry. If you're innocent, you won't burn."

You have only a few moments before your fate is sealed. Maybe the guards can help you.

If you ask the guards to tell you the riddle of the Forbidden Castle, turn to page 17.

If you ask them about what sort of a trial you will have, turn to page 20.

Life with Garth may not be easy, or even safe, but he is a good friend, and you prefer the dangers of the forest to those of King Henry's court, so you join Garth in his forest kingdom.

He teaches you to hunt and fish. In the evenings, the two of you sit around the fire, and he tells stories of knights and dragons until you fall asleep dreaming of days gone by with your family and friends, hundreds of years in the future.

One day Garth turns to you and says, "You have grown quick and strong, and wise in the ways of the forest. It's time for you to decide what sort of life you want to live. If you would like a dangerous life, where you might find fame and fortune, you could enter the court of Rufus, the Mad King of Hereford. Or, if you wish, you can remain in the forest with me!"

If you choose to enter the court of Rufus the Mad, turn to page 21.

If you choose a life in the forest, turn to page 24.

Garth wishes you good luck as you shake hands and say goodbye.

As you trudge along the dusty road, your heart is lightened by the sight of flowering trees, the cheerful songs of birds, and the smells of the sweet summer air.

The afternoon sun is hot when you reach a broad, sloping meadow. You can see Cotwin Castle perched on the next hill. Its high stone walls and tall towers look like a scene from a picture book.

A bugle sounds as you approach the ramparts. The great oak gate swings open, and three knights gallop forth. They rein in their horses beside you. Without a word, one of them lifts you up on his horse, while another prods you with his sword.

Turn to page 10.

14

You follow the road for what feels like miles, wondering whether you will ever find your way to Cotwin Castle, or even find food and shelter by nightfall.

The sun is beginning to set when a traveler comes riding toward you, his cloak billowing behind him.

"Where are you headed?" he calls to you as he reins in his horse. You like his warm brown eyes, and the impish expression on his weather-beaten face.

"I'm looking for Cotwin Castle. Am I heading the right way?" you ask.

"Indeed, you have been heading the wrong way," he says. "But that is a good thing for you. If you were ever to reach Cotwin Castle, they would surely throw you in the dungeon. Because of the clothes you are wearing, they would think you are possessed by evil spirits!"

Evil spirits! You are surprised that anyone could imagine you to be possessed by evil spirits. Then you remember that in medieval times evil spirits were often blamed for unusual happenings.

"What am I to do?" you ask.

"Just keep going. You are only a mile or so from a fishing village. When you get there, ask for Stephen. Tell him that his brother Luke sent you. You can stay with him and his wife. They will teach you how to catch any fish in the sea."

You call your thanks to Luke as he rides off, waving over his shoulder. You continue on your way, and soon reach a hilltop. Although it's nearly dark, you can see the fishing village below—no more than a dozen houses, each with a little garden—nestled by the harbor. Beyond it lies the blue-gray sea. You can see three small boats sailing homeward with the day's catch of fish.

You think about the life ahead of you—a simpler life than the one you thought you would have—without books or TV or movies, planes or cars, or a million other things you took for granted. On the other hand, here there is no pollution, no car wrecks, no bombs. And there will be plenty of excitement fishing and sailing.

Will life be better, or worse, than in your own century?

The End

"Good afternoon," you say. "I am a traveler from a strange land. Can you tell me where I could find food and shelter?"

The woman nods. "Follow me."

You fall into step next to the cart, wondering where she is going.

"Could you tell me what year it is?" you ask.

"Either 1052 or 1152," she says. "I never can remember myself."

You soon reach a tiny stone house at the edge of the woods. She leads you inside and motions you to sit down on a crude oak bench.

"You wonder who I am." She speaks with a cackling voice. "I am called Madame Leeta. I have prophetic powers, and I can tell that *you* have prophetic powers."

"Me?"

"You have a magic disk!" She points to your wrist. You realize that your watch must look magical to her!

"And *you* can see into the future," she continues.

You cannot help but nod your head, for at that moment you *were* looking into the future—thinking of your own home and your own time.

Turn to page 26.

"Please," you ask the two guards, "tell me the riddle of the Forbidden Castle!"

The taller one looks down at you—a stupid grin on his face—and pushes you through the crowd of people gathered in the courtyard. Knights and ladies in colorful robes are laughing and calling to each other.

In the center of the courtyard is a pile of wood stacked around a pole. A man stands next to the pole, holding a coil of rope in one hand and a knife in the other.

The tall guard leans toward you. "The Lord Chancellor will allow a final request before you are tied to the stake." He points to a man, whose dark gray cloak reaches to his ankles.

"May I make a last request?" you ask.

The chancellor looks at you coldly. "What is it?"

"Tell me the riddle of the Forbidden Castle."

"Little good it will do you," he says. "But it is a simple enough request."

He steps closer and looks at you curiously. Then he says:

"Somewhere south, where it is colder,
Where that which falls stays where it is,
You'll find what isn't what it is."

As you stand there, trying to figure out the riddle, the executioner steps forward with his coil of rope. You have only a minute left to live. Escape is impossible.

Go on to page 19.

Suddenly, the guards press you up against the stake. The rough, prickly rope pulls tight against your waist.

You must say something *now*.

If you ask for a little time to solve the riddle, turn to page 25.

If you say, "Stop! I have the solution to the riddle!" turn to page 28.

"What will happen at the trial?" you ask.

"Do not worry," one of the guards replies. "If you are not in league with the devil you will go free."

They lead you out into the courtyard. It is filled with knights and ladies, except for a large area in the middle where a pile of wood is neatly stacked.

"How does this trial proceed?" you ask one of the guards.

"It is simple," he says. "They tie you to the stake and light the fire. If you are guilty, you will burn; if you are innocent, you will not be harmed."

You try to run for it, but the guards quickly grab you. Step by step they march you to your doom.

The End

"I'm grateful for all you've done for me," you tell Garth, "but now I think I'd like to see more of the world. I'm willing to take my chances with Rufus, the Mad King."

"I admire your courage," says Garth. "Rufus may like you, and then again he may not, or he may like you one day and hate you the next. Some say he is generous, some say he is mean. You will soon find out."

For three days Garth travels with you through the forest. When you reach a road that runs alongside a crystal-clear lake, Garth stops and shakes your hand. "Follow this road for a mile or so, and you will reach Fiddlegate, the castle of Rufus the Mad."

You bid him farewell, and start along the road. You miss the company of your friend, but you're happy to feel the warm sun on your back, and to smell the fresh, clean air of the pine forest.

The sun is high overhead when you find yourself at the top of a ridge. Ahead of you is a beautiful green valley. Beyond it is a great castle, with a stone tower which seems to be leaning slightly to one side. As you approach the front entrance, you notice that some of the walls are crumbling and the drawbridge is down. You would think the castle deserted were it not for smoke rising from the courtyard and the cows grazing in a nearby field.

Go on to page 22.

As you stand before the drawbridge, wondering whether to cross it, a bugle blows. After a few minutes two guards appear at the entrance. They lead you to the large, sunlit courtyard. The yard is covered with broken slate tiles. Clumps of weeds and shrubs poke out of the ground.

Turn to page 30.

You stay with Garth, and live in the forest. You become strong and tough, and you learn to make the best of the bad and enjoy the good.

Over the years, others join you and Garth. Some of them are serfs who have run away from their masters; others are knights who did not wish to spend their lives fighting for the king.

By the time you grow up, Garth has grown too old to live the rough life of the forest. You become the leader of the clan. You make a deal with King Henry to protect travelers passing through the forest. In return he gives you and your friends a castle of your own.

It's not the sort of life you expected, but it's as good as you could hope to find hundreds of years before your birth!

The End

"If you will just give me a little time," you say, "I think I can solve the riddle."

The guards laugh in your face.

The chancellor's mouth twists into a cruel smile. "A little time will not do you any good," he says. "You could not solve that riddle in a hundred years!"

The executioner flips a rope over your head and lashes you to the stake, and your last hope flickers out as the flames leap up around you.

The End

Madame Leeta looks at you intently. "I shall now tell you the riddle of the Forbidden Castle. Not more than a year ago, it was—an old monk visited King Henry and told him of a remote castle with four ivory towers. He called it the Forbidden Castle, and he told the king that if he conquered this castle, he would rule all of Europe! The king asked how he could reach the castle. But the monk's only answer was to give the king this riddle:

> *"Somewhere south, where it is colder,*
> *Where that which falls stays where it is,*
> *You'll find what isn't what it is."*

"Since then, the king has spread news of the riddle throughout all of England, in the hope that someone could solve it. He has offered half the kingdom of Wales to anyone who can show him the way! The Baron von Sal, whose lands lie in Alsace, is determined to find the Forbidden Castle and win the reward, and he has engaged me to help him."

"Have you any idea where the castle is?" you ask.

Madame Leeta stares at you with glittering eyes. "We know that the castle lies to the south, so we must cross the English Channel and journey through France. Surely, with your magic powers aiding my own we shall solve the riddle, and then great riches will be ours."

You are tempted to set out with Madame Leeta and the baron. You are curious to see the Forbidden Castle. And it would be nice to be rich. On

the other hand, you know that you don't have any magic powers, just a wristwatch. How can you expect to solve the riddle? Besides, you are worried about how to get back to the twentieth century. Maybe you could find an entrance to the Cave of Time near the field where you suddenly arrived in medieval England.

If you say you'll go with Madame Leeta in search of the castle, turn to page 32.

If you say, "No, thanks, I'm more interested in trying to find my way home," turn to page 33.

"Stop! I have the solution to the riddle!"

The executioner laughs. He waves his lighted torch before your eyes. Suddenly the chancellor steps forward. "Stop the execution!" he says in a loud voice.

"But," the executioner cries, "the prisoner is stalling for time."

"That may be," says the chancellor, "but the prisoner is like none we've seen before. Perhaps this is a wizard. This stranger may be the one person who can answer the riddle."

The knights and ladies begin to chant—*"To the stake! To the stake!"*

But the chancellor leads you out of the courtyard and through an archway, beyond which is a large oak door guarded by two men with heavy swords and shields. One of them opens the door, and the chancellor leads you to a large octagonal room lighted by casement windows over each of the rough stone walls. At the far end of a long oak table sits King Henry himself. He looks at you curiously as he strokes his long, pointed beard. "We have never been so happy as when we learned that you have the solution to the riddle," he says. "So, tell us what it is!"

You have been trying desperately to think of a solution. You think of the first line of the riddle—*"Somewhere south, where it is colder."* At least you have a couple of ideas. Normally it will be warmer, not cooler, if you go south. But the mountains may be cooler, even though farther south, and, of course, the coldest place of all is the South Pole!

"Well?" The king leans forward impatiently.

If you say, "The Forbidden Castle is to the south, but high in the mountains, where it is colder," turn to page 34.

If you say, "The Forbidden Castle is to the south, on the way to the South Pole," turn to page 36.

Again, the bugle sounds. More guards appear. They surround you and march you through the central arch, and then open ranks as a short, fat man waddles toward you. He wears a blue velvet robe and a golden crown on his bald head. Behind him is a very thin man wearing a pointed cap and bells. Surely this must be King Rufus and his court jester!

A guard steps forward. "King Rufus has deigned to look at you."

You bow. "King Rufus, I am honored to visit your court."

"*Silence!* I did not ask you to speak!" says the king. Turning to the jester, he says, "Stillwell, what say you of this intrusion into our royal court?"

" 'Tis a sour sorrow, to us all and all us two," says Stillwell.

The king scowls and says nothing.

The guard points a long, bony finger in your face. "Well, what have you to say for yourself?"

You feel you should say something, but you wonder if it would be wiser to wait until the king himself asks a question.

If you decide to speak, turn to page 37.

If you remain silent, turn to page 39.

You agree to help Madame Leeta find the Forbidden Castle. Soon afterward, there is a knock at the door. It swings open, and a man walks in. His face is very pale, as though he had never been out in the sun. Behind him, through the open door, you see a fine black steed and a small chestnut horse.

"Ah, Baron von Sal—you are early," says Madame Leeta.

The man points to you. "Who is this?"

"A young soothsayer, who can help us solve the riddle of the Forbidden Castle."

"What makes you think so?"

"Show him the magic disk," she demands.

You hold out your watch. The baron bends over and looks at it a moment. He nods gravely. "Then come at once; a boat is already waiting to take us to France."

Madame Leeta rests a long, bony hand on your shoulder. "I knew you would come with us. The three of us shall find the Forbidden Castle, and half the kingdom of Wales shall be ours!"

Turn to page 48.

After leaving Madame Leeta you try to retrace your steps back to the field where you first found yourself. Following a trail through the forest, you come to the hut of a woodsman who gives you food and drink.

"Where are you bound?" he asks.

"I came here from another country and another century through the Cave of Time. I'm trying to find the entrance so I can return to my own time and my own home. Do you know of it?"

You wonder if the woodsman will laugh at your strange story, but he nods his head and replies, "You're not the first one to visit from another time and place. Since you arrived here, you have walked in a circle. The Cave of Time is almost beneath us. I could show you a tunnel that leads to it."

"I would be most grateful," you say.

"I do not know how grateful you should be," he says. "You might find yourself in a time when the world had turned to fire, or to ice!"

You are happy to have learned how to get back to the Cave of Time, but, now that you know where it is, you wonder whether it wouldn't be fun to stay in medieval England awhile. Maybe you can solve the riddle and find the Forbidden Castle.

If you decide to take the tunnel back into the Cave of Time, turn to page 40.

If you decide to stay in medieval England, turn to page 41.

"The Forbidden Castle is to the south," you say, "but high in the mountains, where it is colder."

The king begins to pace around the room. Your heart is pounding. Will he praise you, or send you to your death?

Suddenly he turns, smiling. "There is wisdom in what you say. I know that in the south of France there are mountains higher than any in England, and their tops are covered with snow, while flowers bloom in the valleys below. Now what is the rest of the solution?"

You think of the next line of the riddle: *Where that which falls stays where it is,* but you can hardly even guess at the solution. Could it have something to do with the setting sun? The sun falls below the horizon, yet really stays where it is. . . .

If you say, "The second line has to do with the setting sun," turn to page 42.

If you say, "We must go to the southern mountains; then I will be able to tell you," turn to page 43.

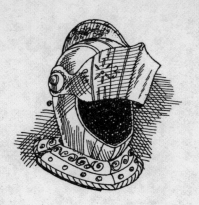

"The Forbidden Castle is to the south," you say, "on the way to the South Pole, where it is cold!"

The king rises, his face reddening with anger. "What nonsense are you telling me? What is this South Pole you speak of?"

Suddenly you realize that the South Pole can't possibly mean anything to the king. It won't be reached for hundreds of years! You try to answer, but the king roars at his guards. They pick you up like a sack of potatoes, and carry you through the door.

"Prepare for execution!" the king calls. "And be quick about it!"

The End

You look the king in the eye. "I would not bring sorrow. I mean no harm."

Stillwell jumps up and down. "He disobeyed your highness's command to be silent."

"Indeed he did." The king's face is red with anger. "Take this impudent youth to the tower!"

Two guards lay hold of you and drag you out of the courtyard. Once outside, one of them glares at you sternly. The other guard starts laughing, yet it is not a cruel laugh—his blue eyes are sparkling.

"The king does not know it," he says, "but the tower steps have long since crumbled away. We have not been able to enter the tower for years!"

"Then what will happen to me?"

"Why, you will escape, of course!" says the other guard with a laugh. Surprised and pleased by their rough kindness, you laugh too!

The guards give you a pack filled with bread and cheese and fruit. They also give you directions to Cotwin Castle. "May you have better luck in King Henry's court. At least he is not mad."

And so, you cross the drawbridge of Fiddlegate Castle and set out for Cotwin Castle.

Turn to page 14.

You're afraid to disobey the king, so you say nothing.

"Well," the king shouts. "Can't you speak?"

Before you can answer, the jester says, "I suggest you teach this youth a lesson!"

"Stillwell, only a fool like you would surely know what not to do!" says King Rufus. "Why haven't I locked you up in the tower?"

"Because, your majesty," says Stillwell, "if you were to lock me up, it would mean you'd made a mistake when you appointed me. Since you are perfect, you cannot make a mistake. Therefore, you cannot lock me up."

The king scowls and paces up and down. Finally he turns to you.

"You have fallen into my favor," he says.

"It would have been better to have fallen in the moat," says Stillwell.

The king smacks Stillwell over the head with the flat side of his sword. Turning to you he says, "If you agree to serve in my court, I shall make you one of my ministers!"

The king seems to have taken a liking to you. He's mad, all right, yet there may be method to his madness. Maybe he would even help you find the Forbidden Castle.

If you dare ask King Rufus to help you find the Forbidden Castle, turn to page 44.

If you agree to serve in his court, turn to page 45.

40

The woodsman shows you the tunnel that leads to the Cave of Time. You thank him for his help. Then, summoning your courage, you crawl in through the narrow entrance.

You shiver in the cold damp air as you inch your way along the dark, musty passageway that winds down into the depths of the earth. Suddenly you are falling, faster and faster, falling into the future!

The time in the future toward which you are falling has not yet come. But it will, and, when it does, your adventure will continue.

So it is only for a while that this is

The End

You agree that returning to the Cave of Time may not be such a good idea, and ask the woodsman if he knows the way to King Henry's court. The woodsman gives you directions to Cotwin Castle. You thank him for his kindness and set out on your journey.

Soon, heavy gray clouds begin to fill the sky. The wind blows harder. The sky darkens. You hear thunder in the distance. As you start across a broad field, sheets of rain suddenly pour down. You run to the shelter of a big pine tree. If only there were a house nearby! You have no rain gear and no place to go. In a minute there is thunder and lightning everywhere around you. . . .

If only you had remembered never to stay under a tree in an open field during a thunderstorm, your story would not have come so quickly to

The End

You look the king in the eye and try to sound as if you know what you're talking about. "We see the sun fall below the horizon when it sets, because the Earth is turning. The sun itself stays where it is!"

"What do you mean, *the Earth turns?*" The king points his finger at you. "You would try to make a fool of me! What you speak is heresy. Anyone can see that the Earth does not move, but it is the sun that travels around the Earth every day!"

If only you could show the king he is wrong, but the guards quickly seize you and drag you back to the dungeon. You wonder if you'll ever get out.

You don't.

The End

"We must go to the southern mountains," you say. "Then I will be able to tell you."

The king frowns. He heaves a sigh and says, "Very well. I shall provide a ship which will take you to France—a day and a half's voyage from Dover, given a fair wind. There shall go with you the Earl of Kent and three of my best knights. Meanwhile, I shall gather my army together—enough men to conquer any castle—and we shall follow within the week. Soon all of Europe will be mine!" He smiles a broad smile. Then, pointing a finger at you, he says, "But if you do not find the Forbidden Castle, I will see you hang from the tallest tree in England!"

Taking care to speak in the manner of the court, you say, "Never fear, my lord, I shall find this castle before the next full moon. Then, as the monk foretold, all Europe shall do homage to your sword!"

"Well spoken," says the king. "Now, make ready, lords, knights, and vassals. We journey to France!"

Turn to page 57.

Looking the king straight in the eye, you say, "I thank you humbly for offering me such an honor, your highness, but I wish to find the Forbidden Castle. Would you help me?"

The king shakes a finger at you. "Impudent youth! I am KING! You are my subject. I don't help my subjects. They *serve* me!"

"Well, *I* can help you. I can win half the kingdom of Wales by finding the Forbidden Castle. Help me and I'll give you half of my kingdom."

"Half your kingdom? I'll take half again as much as a half," says the king.

"I'll give you half of half again as much as half," you quickly reply.

"Call the royal mathematician," says the king to Stillwell. Then he looks at you as he strokes his long, droopy mustache. "You may have wit enough to find the Forbidden Castle. Tomorrow we shall leave at sunrise. *And by our deeds, Rufus shall be king of Wales!*"

The trumpeters blow their horns, and everyone bows as the king struts out of the royal courtyard. You stand there wondering whether you and he will find the Forbidden Castle. Perhaps the world will be better off if you don't!

The End

"I would be honored to serve in your court, my lord."

"Very good," says the king. "Tonight we shall have a banquet in my honor to welcome you."

Stillwell leads you up a spiral staircase to your new quarters—a tiny room with stone walls, and nothing more than a bed of straw and a hole in the wall for a window.

Your bed is almost as hard as the floor, but you lie down for a nap, for it's been a long time since you've had a good night's sleep. It seems no more than a minute later when you are awakened by a knock on the door.

"Who is it?"

"A page, sent to say the banquet is about to begin!"

The page leads you down the long spiral stairs to the great banquet hall. Peering through the archway, you can see that most of the guests are already seated. Your mouth waters at the sight and smell of roast goose, onions, and gravy. As you start to enter the hall a great hulk of a man blocks your way.

"You may not enter!" he says.

"But the king himself invited me!"

"The king did not invite you."

"What do you mean?" you ask. "Who are you to contradict me?"

"The Minister of Contradiction!" he replies.

"What kind of title is that?"

Go on to page 47.

"It is my job," he says. "Too many people in this kingdom were contradicting each other, so the king banned it. He has decreed that all contradicting in the kingdom shall be done by me!"

"Is everything you say a contradiction?"

"NO! The king has ordered me to contradict everything that is said by anyone but him."

"Then I can *not* come to the banquet!" you say.

"Oh, yes you can!" he shouts.

He steps back a moment, and you dash into the hall and quickly take an empty seat at the grand table. On your left is an old knight with a long, sad face; on your right is a woman wearing a white dress adorned with lace.

"Who are you?" you ask the woman.

"I am the Lady in Red," she says.

"But your dress is white."

"How dare you contradict me?" she says. "Only the Minister of Contradiction can do that."

Turn to page 51.

After a rough channel crossing and a fortnight's travel across the French countryside, you and Madame Leeta and the Baron von Sal have finally reached the south of France. The mountain trail you are climbing is steep, and you are all breathing hard under the weight of your packs.

"Are you sure the castle is in the mountains?" the baron demands.

"Of course!" Madame Leeta snaps. "That's the only explanation for the first line of the riddle—*somewhere south, where it is colder.* If you go south, it gets warmer, *unless* you go into the mountains!"

Suddenly she stops and glares at you. "But now it is time for you to tell us the solution to the second line of the riddle—*where that which falls stays where it is.*"

"Yes," says the baron. "It is time for you to use your magic disk!"

You glance at your watch, pretending that it might be able to tell you something other than what time it is.

Should you admit that you really have no magic powers, or should you bluff and hope that somehow you will solve the rest of the riddle and find the Forbidden Castle?

If you admit that you don't think you can solve the riddle, turn to page 52.

If you tell the others not to worry, that you'll solve the riddle soon, turn to page 53.

50

You step into the cave, then wait for your eyes to adjust to the darkness. But Michelle goes on a few feet ahead. Suddenly she cries out. "Help, I'm sliding!"

You grab her arm and try to pull her up, but now you're both falling . . . falling. . . .

It is broad daylight. You and Michelle are both sitting in a field. There is a paved road nearby. A Greyhound bus is going by. A big tractor-trailer is right behind it. *Whoosh,* an oil truck whizzes by.

Michelle screams. "What are those monsters? What a noise! It is horrible!"

"Everything's OK," you say, as you look across the road at the familiar sign that makes you wonder how Michelle would go for a Big Mac and a shake.

The End

Turning to the knight on your left, you ask, "And who are you, sir?"

"The Minister of Laughter," he says with a laugh.

"What does that mean?"

"I decide what is laughable and what is not." He frowns.

You cannot help but laugh.

The minister reddens. "How dare you laugh without my permission?"

At that moment the king stands up and calls for silence. "We welcome a new member of the court." Pointing at you, he says, *"Rise."*

You stand up, and the king unrolls a long scroll. "Hmm, we have just appointed a Minister of Craftiness, a Minister of Happiness, a Minister of Inaction, and a Lady of Ladies in Waiting. There are only two openings left. Tell us which position you would prefer. Would you rather be the Minister of Guesswork, or the Minister of Sanity?"

You look around, hardly able to believe what the king has said. Only now do you fully understand why he is called the Mad King. Absurd as it is, you can see you'll have to pick one job or the other.

If you say you'd rather be the Minister of Guesswork, turn to page 60.

If you say you'd rather be the Minister of Sanity, turn to page 61.

"I really don't think I can solve the riddle," you say.

"You impostor!" the baron cries. He lunges at you, but you are already running down the mountain. He races after you, and, as you look back, you see him trip over a rock and crumple to the ground. In a moment he is up again and limping after you, but you know that he'll never catch you!

You continue down the mountain, following the sound of church bells until you reach the tiny village in the valley below. There you find refuge with a kind family. They offer you food and shelter in exchange for your promise to tend their sheep and goats.

And so you begin a new life in which you resolve each day that, when you grow up, you will climb the mountains and find the Forbidden Castle. Only then will you be ready to return to the Cave of Time.

The End

"Don't worry," you say. "I'll solve the riddle soon."

The baron grumbles, but you pay no attention to him as you lead your companions higher and higher up the mountain trail. If you can only get to the top, you'll be able to see for miles in all directions.

You keep climbing. It's getting cold, and you seem nowhere closer to the top. You pause to rest, not daring to look the baron in the eye, and at that moment you hear, very faintly, a rushing sound. Is it the wind, or is it water?

"Follow me," you say, and you start climbing toward the sound. Madame Leeta and the baron follow eagerly. You cannot be sure where you are headed, but at least you are getting somewhere.

Go on to page 54.

54

You walk along the side of the curving mountain path. Soon you come to a clearing. From here you can see a spectacular waterfall, and beyond that the gleaming white walls, the four towers of the Forbidden Castle!

Turn to page 56.

You and Madame Leeta and the baron hurry over the rocks, and continue along the steep, twisting trail. Finally, almost breathless, you reach the castle gate. A tiny woman dressed in a long gray habit comes forth to meet you.

"I am Sister Anna," she says, "and I welcome you."

"Who is the ruler of this castle?" demands the baron.

"There is no ruler. The castle is tended by the Sisters of Hope," the woman replies. "It is used only as a refuge for the poor and sick."

"Ah!" the baron exclaims. "Then King Henry will have no trouble conquering it. As the monk foretold, he shall become ruler of all of Europe, and I shall become ruler of half of Wales!"

"He *could* conquer it," Sister Anna says gently, "but he will not. To do so would violate the code of chivalry, and he would soon be besieged by all the princes and knights of Europe."

"Achh," the baron cries. "She is right! King Henry will never rule Europe, and I shall never rule Wales! We have journeyed here for nothing! . . . nothing! . . . nothing! . . ."

The baron turns and starts down the trail. Madame Leeta runs after him, screaming, "Stop! Stop! I led you here, and now you must pay me!"

Sister Anna smiles at you. "You have traveled a long way. Stay with us for a while. Listen, observe, and meditate, and you will find your journey worthwhile."

Turn to page 66.

You spend half of the next day floating down the Thames River on the royal barge. It docks in London, and though you are eager to see the ancient city, the Earl of Kent has other plans. He swings you up onto his horse and begins riding toward the southern shore.

The smell of the fresh sea breeze and the flocks of gulls circling overhead tell you that you have arrived in Dover, where one of King Henry's ships is waiting to take you across the English Channel.

You are glad to be safe for the moment. But you keep thinking about what will happen to you if you can't find the Forbidden Castle. The more you think about it, the more you think you'd better escape.

Early the next morning, you, the earl, and three of his knights set sail on one of the royal ships. The voyage is a smooth one, and shortly before noon the next day, you step onto the fertile soil of France.

The Earl of Kent and his knights mount their powerful war-horses. You are ordered into the back of a wooden cart. Though the ride is bumpy and you would rather be on one of the horses, you begin to enjoy the beautiful countryside.

It is late afternoon when you come to a tavern. "We will stop here," the earl calls to the driver. "It is time to load our casks with good French wine. You will wait here; we shall not be long."

Go on to page 59.

They step inside, and you are alone with the driver. He climbs down and walks ahead to check the horses' harness. As he tightens a leather strap, you realize this may be your only chance to escape.

You survey the scene around you. Open pastureland lies on both sides of the road, and there is no place to hide, unless you make it to the bridge a hundred yards or so down the road—the land beyond it is thickly wooded.

If you decide to jump out and run for it, turn to page 62.

If you decide to seize the reins and urge the horses onward, turn to page 63.

"I would like to be Minister of Guesswork," you say.

The assembled lords and ladies clap their hands and cheer.

The king pounds on the table to silence them. "Good choice," he says. "One thing I have learned in this life is that no one can be sure of anything. Therefore we need someone who will guess at everything."

Again the lords and ladies cheer, and again the king bangs on the table until everyone is silent. Then he frowns, and wiggles a finger at you. "But I warn you that I expect the highest standards of performance from my ministers. Are you absolutely sure that you are capable of serving in this high position?"

You think a moment, and then reply, "I *guess* so."

The lords and ladies cheer.

"Well said!" cries the king. "You will make a fine Minister of Guesswork!"

The Lady in Red and the Minister of Laughter pat you on the back as you begin your dinner. You reflect that, if you stay in the mad kingdom, you will soon be as crazy as everyone else. But the roast lamb and peach pie are the best you've ever eaten. Maybe Rufus is not as crazy as all the other kings and lords who spend their lives fighting each other.

The End

"I'll be Minister of Sanity," you say in a loud, clear voice.

Your statement is met with groans and moans. Some of the lords and ladies begin to cry. Others throw up their hands in protest.

The king stands up; his face is pale. "I only said that as a joke—yet you accept it? This is near treason. We have never had a Minister of Sanity, and never will. It would undermine the very principles on which our kingdom is founded."

"We must not have it!" cries the knight sitting near you. "Send this felon from our midst!"

"It's time for a hanging," says another.

"To the stake!" a lady shouts.

"This is madness!" you cry.

Everyone rises and cheers.

"Ah, that is what we want to hear!" says the king. "What you say is worthy of us all, and of you, too. Henceforth you shall be Minister of Madness, the most important minister in the kingdom!"

"Three cheers for our new minister," yells Stillwell, the jester.

Standing, you bow and thank the lords and ladies and the king. "I'll do my best," you say, "to uphold the king—to laugh at sadness, cry at smiles, and keep this kingdom free from logic, sense, and all that's wise."

The End

You jump out of the cart and race down the road. The bridge up ahead spans a swiftly flowing river. The woods beyond it should offer you a good hiding place. But maybe you could throw Henry's men off the track by doubling back and hiding behind the tavern itself.

If you try to make it across the bridge, turn to page 65.

If you run behind the tavern until you can decide what to do next, turn to page 67.

You reach forward, grab the whip from the side of the cart, and take the reins. You crack the whip overhead, and the horses lunge forward, knocking the driver to the ground. As the heavy wooden wheels roll past, he scrambles for the side of the cart. You bring the whip down again, shouting, but the driver has climbed into the cart. Suddenly, one burly hand is on your shoulder; the other grabs the reins and slows the horses from their run. You are filled with dread as he steers the cart back to the tavern where the knights are waiting.

"So, my little friend," says the earl, "you would betray the king. Our search for the Forbidden Castle will continue—as soon as you are hanged!"

The rest of your adventure is too sad to tell.

The End

You run as fast as you can. As you reach the bridge, you look back toward the tavern. The Earl of Kent and his knights are galloping toward you, their swords drawn.

You force yourself to run even faster. Your heart is pounding. As you start across the narrow bridge, you hear the horses right behind you. And you *jump!*

Your right leg hits a jagged boulder. Then you feel only the shocking numbness of the icy water. You struggle to keep your head above water. You gasp for air. The racing current sweeps you downstream. Again and again the swirling black water pulls you under.

You are barely conscious now. The current has swept you against a fallen tree. The water is calmer. You work your way ashore and crawl up the steep muddy slope. As you reach the tall grass along the bank, you collapse. Your leg is bleeding, and you feel so exhausted and bruised that you hardly care whether or not you're alive.

That's a good thing, because in a minute you won't be.

The End

The Sisters of Hope give you a room of your own. Each day they tell you wonderful stories of kings and knights and dragons. You learn to weave tapestries and play the lute. You swim in the sparkling pool beneath the waterfall, and ride the mountain ponies. But, as good as life is, you become more and more homesick.

"What is troubling you?" Sister Anna asks one day.

"I dream of finding the entrance to the Cave of Time so that I can return to my home in the twentieth century."

"It need not be a dream," she says and hands you a tiny wooden pipe. "If you blow on this reed, it will summon the unicorn. You need only follow it, and it will lead you to the Cave of Time."

Your eyes open wide. "But I thought unicorns never really existed."

"Oh, but they do," she replies, "though you will find it difficult to believe when you return to your twentieth century. You may not even believe you visited the Forbidden Castle, and yet you will not forget it. As you dreamed of your own home here, so will you dream of the Forbidden Castle when you return to your own time."

The End

You dash around the side of the tavern, keeping as low as you can, so as not to be seen through the casement windows. As you round the rear corner, you almost crash into a young girl with the longest braids you've ever seen.

"What are you running from?" she asks, but she gives you no time to answer. "My name is Michelle. I live in the tavern. Come, I will show you where to hide."

You follow her down a steep flight of stone steps, through a dark passageway, and into a small room filled with casks of wine. The only light comes from a few cracks between the stones in the wall.

"I will bring you food and milk when it is safe," she says. Then she turns and hurries up the stairs.

You sit in the cellar, wondering what will become of you. When will Michelle return? You would like to sneak upstairs to get some food, but you don't dare. King Henry's knights will surely be looking for you.

A few minutes later the door swings open, and Michelle steps in, carrying a plate heaped with food.

"Lamb, pears, and fresh bread," she says. "The cook is a friend of mine. I've good news, too. The English knights have left. They think you are hiding in the woods."

Go on to page 68.

While you eat, you tell Michelle about everything that has happened since you arrived in England hundreds of years before your birth.

She listens intently, and when you have finished she says, "It is a strange story you tell, but I am very glad you have come. My parents died when I was a small child. The innkeeper said I could live at the inn if I swept the floors and helped the cook. Now he works me night and day, and beats me if I complain. I have been afraid to run away alone, but we can go together."

"How?"

"The cook will give us packs of food. I will take blankets and two good horses. The moon will be full tonight. We will ride the road south. There is just one more thing. You cannot expect to hide from anyone in those clothes. See what I've brought?" She hands you a small bundle. "Put these on!"

It is near midnight when Michelle comes to get you. A few moments later the two of you gallop down the road, free!

Turn to page 81.

You and Michelle follow the trail to the west, which winds around the steep hillside. The sun is beginning to set when you see a rambling building made of stones and logs. Wild flowers and ferns are growing on the sod-covered roof. Goats and sheep graze nearby.

"This must be a monastery," Michelle says, "but look, someone is using it as a farm." As she speaks, a man walks out of the building.

"And who are you?" he asks.

"We are travelers from the north," says Michelle. "And who are *you*?"

"Auguste le Bon," he replies, "late of service to the Prince of Lyon, but now I tend this farm for the Philosopher Knights."

Auguste takes you inside and gives you bread and cheese and warm broth. He tells you that the Philosopher Knights spend most of their time studying philosophy and playing chess, but they are at present visiting the court of the Prince of Lyon, who, it seems, fears an invasion by Henry, King of England.

"Naturally, he has called upon the Philosophers for advice," says Auguste.

Auguste asks if you would like to spend the night, and you and Michelle gratefully accept. In the morning you ask Auguste if he thinks you can safely get past the Dragon of the Ledges.

Go on to page 72.

"I cannot answer that," he says, "for I have never known anyone to try. But I know of a secret trail through No Man's Forest. It is possible to get through safely, though there is great risk. I will be glad to show you the way, if you like. Whichever route you take, you must travel on foot, for the dragon trail is too steep and rugged, and the trail through the forest is sometimes no more than a tunnel through the thorns."

Michelle beckons you aside. "What do you think?" she says.

You're tempted to choose the dragon trail. After all, you're from the twentieth century and you know that dragons never really existed. On the other hand . . .

If you decide to go through No Man's Forest, turn to page 74.

If you decide to take the dragon trail, turn to page 77.

If you decide to wait at the farm until the Philosophers return, turn to page 78.

You and Michelle ride to the east—through forests and meadows, over hills and through valleys.

It is well past midday when you unsaddle your horses and sit in the shade of a towering elm tree to rest and eat.

As you prepare to resume your journey, two men approach on foot. They are dressed in peasant clothes, though one of them wears a gold medallion on his chest.

"Is it far to the southern mountains?" you ask them.

"The mountains are only a day's journey to the south, across the lands of Count Gaston," replies one of the men. "You will find the trails so steep that you will not be able to use your horses, but we shall take care of them for you."

"What do you mean?" Michelle cries.

Suddenly, the men untether your horses!

"What are you doing?" Michelle shouts. *"Stop!"*

But the strangers mount your horses and ride off at a brisk trot. You run after them, but there is no chance of catching up. Your horses are gone for good.

Turn to page 80.

You and Michelle follow Auguste through a forest of towering pines. Late in the day you reach a slow-moving, muddy stream. A huge fallen tree forms a bridge across it. Beyond the stream are the thickest woods you've ever seen.

"You can camp here for the night," says Auguste. "The trail through No Man's Forest begins at the other end of the bridge. If you start out at dawn, and travel at a good pace, you will be safely through the forest by sunset. But do not stop to rest. The snakes come out at night."

Early the next morning you and Michelle carefully cross the bridge and set out on the trail through No Man's Forest. You follow a twisting route which winds around great clumps of thorns and plunges down into gullies and up steep ridges. Each of you carries a stick to brush aside the thorn branches which hang down across the path.

You walk briskly along without rest, until the sun sinks low in the western sky and the forest grows darker. If only you knew how much farther you had to go!

"I am so tired I can barely walk," says Michelle. "Can we stop for just a few moments?"

If you agree to rest for a few minutes, turn to page 116.

If you insist on pushing on, turn to page 118.

"Let's take a chance, and follow the dragon trail," you tell Michelle.

You thank Auguste for his help, and start up the narrow winding trail that leads past the Dragon of the Ledges.

You've been traveling about half a day when Michelle stops, so quickly that you bump into her. Looking ahead, you see that the trail leads into a clearing. Scattered about are piles of bones—whether animal or human you cannot tell. Suddenly, you hear a hiss. A puff of smoke floats toward you from behind a huge boulder at the far end of the clearing.

Michelle clutches your arm. "The dragon! It is just beyond that big rock!"

"In the twentieth century, we don't believe in dragons," you say.

"You are not *in* the twentieth century!" says Michelle. "Believe me, there *are* dragons in this century!"

You stay absolutely still. The hissing continues. Puffs of smoke drift toward you. You try to keep from coughing. You wonder whether you can outrun a dragon. You're scared, but you are also curious.

If you continue on through the clearing, turn to page 82.

If you retreat, turn to page 85.

"Let us wait for the Philosophers to return," you say. Michelle agrees.

When you tell Auguste that you do not wish to go to No Man's Forest, he shakes his head. "Well," he says, "I cannot blame you, for the path I would have shown you is a dangerous one. The truth is that, in this country and in these times, whatever you do, the odds are against you."

For the next two days, you and Michelle help Auguste feed the chickens and milk the goats. At dusk you take one of the dogs and bring the sheep in from the pasture. It's good to have a break in your travels, but you can't stop thinking about the Forbidden Castle. You ask Auguste what he knows about it and he shudders. "Terrible things have happened there. It is best you do not ask."

You are glad when you finally see the Philosophers riding up the road. They are a scragglylooking lot—of all ages and manner of dress—but they introduce themselves politely, and thank you earnestly for helping Auguste take care of the farm.

That evening you sit down to a dinner of mutton and beans. The food is good, but the Philosophers pay no attention to you or Michelle. Instead, they spend the whole meal arguing over whether a waterfall makes a noise when there is no one close enough to hear it. After dinner they retire to their chambers, except for Sir Bertram and Sir Gregory.

"Where are you bound?" asks Sir Bertram.

"To the Forbidden Castle," you reply.

Sir Bertram raises his eyebrows. "Then you

must take the trail past the Dragon of the Ledges. Am I not right, Sir Gregory?''

"Quite so," Sir Gregory replies. "But do not be alarmed—it is simple enough to scare the dragon away. Catch a few mice, put them in a cage, and let them loose in front of the dragon. Then just keep out of its way when it runs.''

"How do you know the dragon will be afraid of mice?'' you ask.

"It is simple, just a matter of logic: all elephants are afraid of mice. Elephants are large animals. Therefore all large animals are afraid of mice. Since dragons are large animals, all dragons must be afraid of mice.''

If you decide to follow Sir Gregory's advice, turn to page 86.

If you decide not to follow Sir Gregory's advice, turn to page 87.

Using the sun as your compass, you and Michelle continue on foot, heading southeast, hoping that you may safely pass through Count Gaston's lands without being seen by his men.

Later that day, after traveling through a pine forest, you are glad to see a broad stream up ahead, and rolling fields beyond it.

"I think we have reached the lands of Count Gaston," says Michelle.

No sooner has she spoken than you hear the howling of a wolf behind you; then another to one side—much closer. And another!

"They are on our trail," says Michelle. "It will not be long before they find us."

As she talks, you look for something to use as a weapon. You pick up a fallen branch and break it in two. Now you have a good club. You can probably defend yourself against a single wolf, but you hear others, much closer! The pack is closing in.

Michelle points to a tall pine with branches reaching almost to the ground. "Quick! Climb up into that tree."

You had the same thought, but another idea occurs to you. If you could walk through the stream for a way, the wolves would lose your scent, and you could escape on the other side of the stream.

If you run to the tree and climb it, turn to page 88.

If you tell Michelle to follow you, and run for the stream, turn to page 89.

For two days you and Michelle ride the trail south, stopping only long enough to get some sleep and let your horses rest.

On the morning of the third day, you reach a fork in the trail, where you meet a shepherd.

"Good morning, friend," you say. "Could you tell us which trail will take us south to the mountains?"

The shepherd looks at you quizzically, and shakes his head. "I could not say, except to say you cannot go south by going south."

"What new riddle is this?" Michelle demands.

"It is no riddle," the shepherd replies, "but a simple truth, for to the south of us lies No Man's Forest, where the trails are blocked by thickets and thorns, and deadly snakes await you underfoot and above, dangling from the trees. So, if you want to go south, you first must go east or west."

"What lies to the west?" you ask.

The shepherd frowns, and says, "The trail to the west winds up around high, rocky hills, where the January wind blows in July and the Dragon of the Ledges waits for foolish travelers."

"And to the east?" asks Michelle.

"To the east are the lands of the Count Gaston, where half the wolves in Europe roam."

You and Michelle exchange glances. "We cannot turn back now," she says. "We must go east or west. They both sound bad to me."

If you head west, turn to page 71.

If you head east, turn to page 73.

"We've come this far," you whisper to Michelle. "I'm not going to turn back now."

As quietly as you can, the two of you pick your way through the bleached white bones, hoping the dragon will not hear you. Michelle regains her courage and follows close behind. But the hissing grows louder. Sparks, glowing cinders, and billowing puffs of smoke fill the air. Looking down, you see the empty eye sockets of a human skull staring up at you. Gritting your teeth, you continue past the rock, steeling yourself to face the dragon.

There before you is a fire of blazing pine boughs. Sitting beside it is an old man with a long, white beard. He holds a blacksmith's bellows to the flames and blows fire and sparks toward you. You jump back just in time to avoid being singed by the leaping flames. He seems too busy to notice you, as he lifts a ram's horn to his mouth and blows an eerie, wailing blast—the terrible sound of the Dragon of the Ledges!

Michelle runs up, laughing.

The old man lays down his bellows and his horn. He stands there—hands outstretched. "You have met the dragon," he says. "You are the first who dared come so close!"

"Ah ha!" says Michelle. "Wait until the Prince of Lyon learns your secret!"

"Please, please." The old man holds out his arms to you. "I am an escaped serf. If they find me, they will hang me."

Go on to page 84.

"We will keep your secret," you say, "if you will just guide us on our way."

"And where are you going?" he asks.

"We are searching for the Forbidden Castle."

The old man looks wistfully upward for a moment. "... *That which falls but does not move* ..." he says, smiling.

"That's part of the riddle!"

"Will you keep my secret if I tell you the answer?"

"Yes!"

"Then follow me."

The old man leads you further along the steep winding trail, up over a high ridge. From the crest the land drops down into a steep gully, and then rises up to become a magnificent snow-capped peak.

He holds a finger to his lips. *"Listen."* You stand there, straining your ears. Across the ravine you can barely hear the faintest rushing sound, as faint as a memory. . . .

"A waterfall!" Michelle exclaims.

The old man smiles. *"That which falls stays where it is!"*

You thank the old man and wish him well, and you and Michelle hurry on along the trail with renewed energy and high spirits.

Turn to page 91.

"I don't want *our* bones lying in that pile," you tell Michelle. "Let's head back the way we came!"

Michelle wastes no time hurrying back down the trail, and you are right behind her.

For a long time neither of you speaks. It looks as if you have given up your best chance to reach the Forbidden Castle. Sad, you descend the narrow, winding trail leading back toward the farm.

The afternoon sun has grown hot when Michelle points out a lake not far off your trail. "Let us go there to rest and get water," she says.

You cut through the woods to the lake, and gratefully sit on a rock and dangle your feet in the cool, clear water.

Then you both notice the same thing—a plume of smoke rising from the opposite shore.

"That looks like a campfire," you say. "Let's see who's there. They might be able to guide us to a trail to the southern mountains."

Turn to page 94.

86

Sir Gregory gives you a box trap and some cheese. You have no trouble catching a couple of mice in the barn, and the next morning you and Michelle set out on your journey. Following Sir Gregory's directions, you head for the dragon trail. But there are many forks and branches along the way, and by mid-afternoon you are totally lost. All you can do is to continue on, hoping to find food and shelter. Finally, cold, hungry, and exhausted, you and Michelle lie down to rest.

Turn to page 96.

You ask Sir Bertram his opinion of Sir Gregory's advice.

He laughs. "Nonsense! Just because all elephants are afraid of mice doesn't mean all large animals are afraid of mice. But if you blow on a goat's horn, the dragon will leave you alone. It must be so, because the Duke of Foussy once saw a dragon outside his castle. He leaned out the window and blew on a goat's horn. Soon afterward the dragon went away!"

If you decide to follow Sir Bertram's advice, turn to page 97.

If you decide to ask one of the other Philosophers, turn to page 99.

88

You climb up the tree, right behind Michelle. In an instant the wolves are below you. They leap up against the tree trunk. You and Michelle are trapped. There is nothing to do but wait.

Hours later, when darkness begins to fall, the wolves are still there. Some of them are napping. One of them quietly licks his paws. Another howls mournfully, while a third wolf sits motionless, staring up at you.

You huddle against the cold through the long, dark night. The early morning light reveals no sign of the wolves, and you are eager to be down from the tree and on your way.

"Shall we continue," asks Michelle, "or wait a couple of hours to make sure they are gone?"

If you say, "Let's go now," turn to page 100.

If you say, "Let's wait a while," turn to page 101.

You and Michelle quickly reach the stream. The water is cold, but you wade easily downstream, for the water hardly rises above your knees. Finally, you feel you've come far enough to lose the wolves.

After picking your way over round, slippery rocks, you emerge on the other side of the stream. Through the woods you can see a freshly ploughed field. You hurry toward it.

You have no sooner reached the field when you hear the pounding of hoof beats. A moment later three horsemen come over a rise, riding straight for you. Two of them look like common knights, but the third has a dome-shaped helmet topped by a sharp-pointed spike. His face is covered by a full, black beard, so that all you can see of him are his steel-gray eyes.

"Who are you to set foot on the lands of Count Gaston?" he demands.

You start to explain, but he interrupts. *"Have you not heard of me?"*

You nod your head.

"Then know that I fear no one. Now, what is your purpose here?"

"We are looking for the Forbidden Castle," Michelle says.

Go on to page 90.

The count laughs. "You are neither wise enough nor strong enough to reach the Forbidden Castle, for it is high in the mountains to the south. You may pass safely through my lands on your journey, or, if you like, I shall permit you to remain here in my service. You will live well, and you will learn more than you could by journeying all over Europe. If you stay, know that it shall be for not one day less than a year! And at the end of that year, if you wish, I, myself, will guide you to the Forbidden Castle!"

"Can you just tell us how to get there?" you ask.

"I have said what I intended to say," the count replies. "You must make your decision now!"

If you continue on through the lands of Count Gaston, turn to page 103.

If you agree to remain in the count's service, turn to page 104.

The trail descending into the ravine is steep and rugged, and you are glad to reach the bottom safely and begin the long climb up the mountainside. When you finally reach the ledge and look straight into the silvery cascade, the waterfall roars in your ears. The pines and ferns glisten with spray. You work your way around to the left of the falls, and climb to a higher ledge.

There it is! Gleaming in the late afternoon sunlight, walls built upon walls—massive blocks of chalk-white stones, and, soaring above them, four ivory towers that seem to pierce the mountain sky. The Forbidden Castle!

"Never have I seen anything so beautiful!" Michelle says.

Then, looking back toward the valley below, you see a line of mounted horses. At least a hundred men are following on foot.

"Michelle, it's King Henry! He must have traced our path!"

Go on to page 92.

"Do you think he can conquer the Forbidden Castle?" she asks.

You and Michelle run still higher, toward the castle. Strange to see, the drawbridge lies open. There aren't even chains or ropes by which it could be raised. A tiny woman wearing a long gray habit comes forth to greet you.

"Welcome! I am Sister Anna."

"Good day, Sister," you say. "Where is the prince who rules this great castle?"

"And why is it called the *Forbidden* Castle?" Michelle adds.

Sister Anna smiles. "There is no prince, nor knights here—only the Sisters of Hope. You see, once a great prince ruled this castle, attended by a splendid court, but a plague swept across the lands and wiped out all the lords and ladies who lived here—every one! For years no one dared to come near, and so it became known as the Forbidden Castle.

"But we vowed not to be afraid of plagues, whether borne by rats, or kings, or knaves. We

came to tend the sick and helpless. Since then, good fortune has come to all who have visited here in friendship."

As Sister Anna is speaking, the third line of the riddle comes to your mind—*"You'll find what isn't what it is."*

"Is this a castle, or isn't it?" you ask.

The sister smiles. "You need only look at it to see that it is a castle," she says. "And yet it is not a castle, with a lord and his vassals, but a refuge for the poor and the helpless. Therefore, *it isn't what it is!"*

You have been so amazed by the sister's story that you have forgotten about King Henry and his army. But now you hear bugles blowing, shouts, and the sound of horses!

Other sisters come forth from the castle. You and Michelle step aside as they form a line to block King Henry and his powerful army.

Turn to page 114.

As you reach the other side of the lake, Michelle stops short. "Listen! Do you hear the music?"

You cut through the woods and slowly creep to the edge of a clearing. Before you are three brightly painted wagons. It is a gypsy camp! Horses, dogs, goats, and chickens are scattered about. A dozen or so people are sitting around a fire. One man shakes a tambourine; another strums a lute. Children are darting in and out, and a woman is dishing up steaming stew from a huge iron kettle.

Near you, a dark-haired boy, a little older than you, is soothing a colt, "Whoa, Lightning. What frightens you?" The colt stares in your direction, and the boy shouts to the others. In a moment the gypsies surround you, all of them talking at once, *"Who are you?" "Where did you come from?" "Where are you going?"*

"We are looking for the Forbidden Castle," says Michelle. The gypsies laugh.

"If it is *forbidden,*" says the boy, "then it cannot be a good thing to find. Why not forget it? Join our band, instead!"

"Yes! Yes!" shout the others.

"But the castle . . .," you begin.

The gypsy boy takes your wrist and stares at your open palm. "You have already faced great danger. If you continue, far greater danger awaits you." He drops your hand and grins. "If you stay with us, you can ride horses, and swim streams, and have more fun than you would have in any castle."

You look at the spirited horse, and then back at Michelle, who has already put on a crimson scarf. "Let us stay here a while," she says.

"All right," you say. "I've always wondered what it's like to be a gypsy."

An older man places the lute in your hand. You pluck the strings, and listen to its rich tones.

"You shall learn to play," says Michelle, "and I shall learn to dance!" She joins the circle of people whirling round the fire to the beat of the tambourine. You begin to pick out a tune on the lute. With each note, the twentieth century drifts farther away.

The End

You wake up, to find yourself lying in a crude bed in a tiny room with walls of straw and clay. Michelle is nearby—still sound asleep. A woman is standing over you. She is dressed in simple peasant clothes. You manage to sit up, though you still feel weak and dizzy. She props a pillow behind you. "Here, drink this. The English knights are searching for you, but I told them that I had not seen anyone who looked like you or your friend. Where, may I ask, were you bound?"

"We were searching for the Forbidden Castle," you say.

"I have heard of the Forbidden Castle," says the woman, "but I have also heard that it only exists in dreams. So you might as well get some more sleep—perhaps you will find it in your dreams!"

You lie back, and quite soon you fall asleep. And you dream of an ivory castle set on a mountain ledge near a waterfall. Its tall, rounded towers gleam in the pink-gold light of the setting sun.

Slowly, you awaken from the dream. You open your eyes. The castle is gone, and so is Michelle and the kindly peasant woman, for, as you can see by looking around, you are right here, back in your own time.

The End

Sir Bertram supplies you and Michelle with a goat's horn, shows you how to blow on it properly, and tells you how to find the trail to the dragon. The next day you set out at dawn, hoping that the trail will lead you safely past the dragon and on to the castle.

You travel on and on, but the trail seems to lead nowhere. You have almost given up hope when you see three knights riding toward you. They rein in their horses.

"You are on the prince's royal hunting ground!" says the leader. "You will come with us!"

They lead you to a great stone house, set on top of a hill, and down a long stone stairway leading to a room below the courtyard. They push you inside and lock the door behind you.

It is pitch dark. You grope around, but you find no other place to sleep that night than the cold stone floor. Lying there in the dark you hear rats scurrying about. One of them nibbles at your ear.

Life never looked so bad.

The End

You and Michelle knock at the chamber of a third Philosopher, Sir René, and find him playing chess with Sir Charles. They listen impatiently while you ask their opinion of Sir Bertram's advice.

"How foolish an argument," says Sir René. "Just because the dragon ran away *after* the duke blew on his horn does not mean he ran *because* the duke blew on his horn. You should ask the stable-keeper, who must know about dragons as well as horses."

"Nonsense!" cries Sir Charles. "The stable-keeper is a peasant, and so would never know the answer. They should journey to the court and ask Count de Rue. He is a man so worthy that he is often seen in the company of the prince!"

"Ah yes, a much better idea. Ask Count de Rue," says Sir René. He moves his rook across the chess board. *"Check!"*

You take Michelle aside. "I think they're all crazy," you whisper. "What do you think?"

"Perhaps," says Michelle, "but they do not seem unkind. One of them may even help us find the Forbidden Castle. If only we knew which one to believe . . ."

If you decide to journey to the court to see Count de Rue, turn to page 105.

If you decide to talk to yet another Philosopher, turn to page 107.

100

You climb down the tree, moving as silently as you can. Michelle follows. You stand there a while, ready to climb back up at any second.

"Let's go," you whisper.

You have almost reached the shallow stream at the edge of the forest when you hear once again the mournful howling of the wolves.

Michelle starts to run toward the stream. You follow close behind. But now you see them—at least a dozen gray wolves, running along on either side of you, closing in. This time there are no trees to climb. You grab a stick to use as a weapon, but there are too many of them, and they are hungry. . . .

The End

After waiting a few hours without seeing or hearing any wolves, you climb down the tree. Michelle follows closely behind. Keeping a sharp watch, you make your way across the stream and cross a meadow. You climb a steep hill. From the top you can see the mountains beyond. One of them is higher than the others. Patches of snow lie in the gullies near its peak.

"We haven't solved the riddle," you say, "but there's a chance that from the top of that mountain we will be able to see the Forbidden Castle."

Late the next day, as you and Michelle wearily climb the steep slope of the mountain, you begin to realize that the distance to the top is much greater than it looked. You doubt whether you can reach the summit. To make matters worse, the higher you climb, the colder it gets. The clouds grow thicker, and the wind blows harder, bringing with it fog and rain that ruin your hopes of glimpsing the Forbidden Castle.

Turn to page 108.

"Thank you for your offer," you tell the count. "We would rather have our freedom."

The count leaps down from his horse, grabs you by your hair, and swings you around. Then he pushes you roughly away, and looks into your pack.

"I see that you have very little food left. Beyond my lands are woods thick with robbers and wolves. You are brave, but you are foolish!"

You start to speak, but the count is already remounting his horse. "Adieu," he cries as he rides briskly away.

One of the knights returns your pack. The other prods you with his lance. "Get moving."

"He could have given us a little more time to think," says Michelle.

"Count Gaston never asks twice," says the knight. *Follow me.*

Turn to page 109.

Fearing that you could never make it to the Forbidden Castle on your own, you and Michelle agree to stay in the service of the count.

You soon learn what it is like to be in the service of Count Gaston. As a page, you must always be ready to assist your lord. Each day you must prepare his clothing, care for his armor, and wait on his table. You even learn to hunt with falcons. Michelle is in training to be a lady of the court. Her time is devoted to music, poetry, and Latin, as well as riding. At the end of the day, there is chess and backgammon for you, and astronomy for Michelle. Then bed. Every day is the same. There is plenty of food, and your master is not unkind, but your heart aches—you long to be free.

One day, about a month later, the count visits you. "What's the matter with you two?" he says. "You eat well, and you are sheltered from the cold winds and rain. You have warm clothes." The count grows angry as he talks. "You are ungrateful for all that I have done for you. Would you rather I had left you to the wolves?"

You bow your head. There is little you can say. The count strides off. You return to your cell and carve another tiny mark in a corner of the thick oak floor. Only 327 days until you and Michelle are free again.

The End

Sir Charles gives you directions through the forest to the palace of the Count de Rue. Early the next morning, you pack as much food and supplies as you can carry, and set out on your journey.

For four days you and Michelle follow first one trail and then another, through woods so dense that you almost never see the sun. Sir Charles's directions seem to make no sense.

At last you admit to each other that you are lost. You wander on and on, hoping to find your way, but the trails you have followed are like passageways in an endless maze.

You and Michelle are never seen again.

The End

You knock on the door of Sir Harold, another Philosopher.

"Come in, come in, come in," he calls.

When you tell Sir Harold what Sir Charles and Sir René advised you, he shakes his head.

"No, no, no, no, no . . . They're *wrong,* for the truth of what a man says does not depend on who he is or who his friends are. Let me tell you what to do: the dragon can be captured by holding a noose outside his cave, because when the dragon comes out he will walk right into the noose."

"Are you *sure* that will work?" you ask.

Sir Harold strokes his beard a few times, as if deep in thought, and says, "Yes, yes, yes . . . absolutely, because it is logical and self-evident. Moreover, it stands to reason, and, finally, it is indisputable!"

If you decide that Sir Harold's advice is probably as good as any, and you might as well follow it, turn to page 110.

If you decide that Sir Harold's advice is absurd, turn to page 112.

Finally, you and Michelle can climb no farther. You stop—cold, weak, wet, hungry, and exhausted.

Suddenly you hear a deep, loud barking.

"What is that?" cries Michelle.

"More wolves! Come on! We've got to find shelter!" But even as you are talking, you see two enormous white wolves running toward you. This time, there's no chance you'll escape.

"They're *dogs!*" shouts Michelle.

And they are—Great Pyrenees mountain dogs! One of them licks Michelle's face—she laughs. The other tugs at your sleeve. You both laugh.

"Michelle, I think they want us to follow them!"

Filled with new energy, you follow the great white dogs over the top of the ridge. Night will soon be upon you, but the sky grows brighter in the west as the storm clouds break. By the time you reach the top of the ridge, the mists have lifted, and the red sun—just about to set—breaks through the clouds.

There, before you, gleaming in the last pink light of the day, is a white stone castle capped by four ivory towers.

You blink and look again. "Michelle, it's the Forbidden Castle!"

Michelle gives you a hug. "What a beautiful sight," she says. "No matter what happens now, I will feel that it was worth the trip!"

"I agree," you say.

The End

Gaston's knight escorts you to the edge of the forest. You and Michelle travel on through the woods, hoping to find food and shelter. Fortunately, you encounter neither wolves nor robbers, but the weather changes. A chill wind blows from the north, and great dark clouds fill the sky.

Suddenly Michelle grabs your arm. "Look—a cave! Shall we take shelter before the storm hits?"

If you continue on, turn to page 113.

If you go into the cave, turn to page 50.

Sir Harold gives you and Michelle a sharp knife and a strong, heavy rope, and you set out for the dragon trail.

You are happy when, by late afternoon, you come upon a little thatched cottage. Hoping to find a place to stay for the night, you knock on the door. It is opened by a slender woman with long blond hair. A sparkling green stone hangs from a chain around her neck. You can't stop looking into her glittering eyes.

"You have traveled far," she says. "Come with me and rest. I shall bring you hot broth."

You and Michelle follow her inside. As you start to warm your hands by the fire, the woman bolts the door. Then, turning toward you, she smiles; it is a strange smile. "Poor things—you do not seem to be able to tell a witch when you see one. Now you will learn quite well as you receive my spell."

"What spell?"

"A spell of forgetfulness, so that you will not remember how you returned to your own time. . . ."

The End

Do you remember?

"I don't think much of Sir Harold's advice," you say. "How about you, Michelle?"

"It sounds foolish to me," she says. "I do not see why we have to take the dragon trail in the first place. There must be other ways to reach the Forbidden Castle!"

You think for a moment and say, "I know what to do. We'll take the dragon trail almost as far as where the dragon lives, and then cut through the forest."

The next morning at sunrise, you and Michelle strap on your packs and leave the sleepy Philosophers. The two of you follow the dragon trail for half a day, and then cut south through the forest, using the sun as your compass. Suddenly you hear a tremendous roar, a thunderclap which rattles your bones, and you feel a fiery blast of air like the flaming breath of a dragon. No, it cannot be—dragons never really lived on Earth! Shielding your face with one arm, you turn to look . . . *too late*.

The End

"I think we'd better push on," you tell Michelle. "If we rest in the cave, we may find ourselves too weak to continue. We must find food before we stop."

"Then let us push on!" says Michelle.

You are soon glad of your decision, for as you walk along, the storm clouds break, and the sun begins to shine; you find delicious berries growing along your way.

Presently, the trail forks to the west and the east. The branch leading to the east is overgrown with thorns and poison ivy.

Turn to page 71.

King Henry's army winds its way up the mountainside. At last the armored troop comes to a halt. King Henry dismounts. He walks up to Sister Anna, draws his sword, and holds it high above his head. The sisters stand motionless before him. Suddenly the king hurls his sword to the ground. "How can I conquer a castle defended by little old ladies?" he roars. "It would violate the code of chivalry!"

Sister Anna steps forward and touches his arm. "And pray, great king," she says, "how would it profit you to conquer this castle? You already have a castle of your own. Were you to rule all Europe, I am sure that you would soon have more problems than pleasures. So stay if you wish; drink our nectar, and eat honey bread; forget about conquests, and go in peace."

The king stares at the castle, and at the mountains and the waterfall. He slowly shakes his head.

"What will I tell my knights?" he says softly. "They will laugh at me for leading them here!"

"Tell them," Sister Anna says with a smile, "that you led them here to teach them a lesson."

King Henry turns towards his followers. He shouts a command, and they turn and start slowly down the mountain.

The sisters invite you and Michelle to stay with them. You gratefully accept their invitation, but you are already thinking of your next journey to search for the entrance to the Cave of Time, for now you wish nothing more than to return to your own century and your own home.

The End

"I could use a rest, myself," you say, as you gratefully sit down on the soft moss beneath a gnarled old tree.

Michelle quickly joins you. "We'd best take only a few minutes," she says.

You lean up against the tree and close your eyes. It seems like only a minute later when you open them again, but at least an hour must have gone by, for the sun has set, and there is barely enough light for you to see the trail ahead. Michelle is sound asleep.

"Quick, wake up!" You shake her and pull her to her feet.

The two of you half-walk, half-run along the trail for a few minutes before the darkness closes in and you are forced to grope your way through the thorns and brambles, trying to stay on the trail. But it doesn't matter any more. All around you, wherever you look, the snakes are coming out.

The End

"We can't stop now," you say. "It will be dark soon."

You hurry along the trail, slowing only to push the thorny branches aside. But darkness comes quickly in No Man's Forest. You strain to see each turn in the trail. Then suddenly it grows lighter up ahead. A few quick steps and you yell for joy—"Michelle, we made it!" Ahead of you is a field of golden grain. On the hillside beyond is a stone cottage. Nearby a peasant woman is hoeing a small garden. You and Michelle run toward her, and she looks up from her work.

"Can you give us some food?" Michelle says. "We are lost and hungry."

"I would like to help you, but I am a poor serf," says the woman. "I work for the lord of the manor; he is a cruel man. Look, there are two of his knights now!" She points to two men riding straight toward you.

Right now you are too weary and hungry to resist.

"What can we do?" Michelle asks.

You look at her and manage to smile. "We've been through a lot, and we've learned a lot. Someday we shall escape. And we shall find the Forbidden Castle!"

The End

ABOUT THE AUTHOR

A graduate of Princeton University and Columbia Law School, EDWARD PACKARD lives in New York City, where he is a practicing lawyer. Mr. Packard conceived of the idea for the Choose Your Own Adventure® series in the course of telling stories to his children, Caroline, Andrea, and Wells.

ABOUT THE ILLUSTRATOR

PAUL GRANGER is a prize-winning illustrator and painter.